Little Nino's PIZZERIA

Karen Barbour

Voyager Books
Harcourt Brace & Company
San Diego   New York   London
Printed in Hong Kong

SPECIAL THANKS TO HERMANN LEDERLE

Library of Congress Cataloging-in-Publication-Data
Barbour, Karen.
Little Nino's pizzeria.
Summary: Tony likes to help his father at their
small family restaurant, but everything changes
when Little Nino's Pizzeria becomes a fancier place.
(1. Restaurants, lunchrooms, etc.—Fiction.
2. Pizza—Fiction. 2. Fathers and sons—Fiction.)
I. Title.
PZ7.B2336Li 1987 (E) 86-32006
ISBN 0-15-246321-6 (pb)

V U T S R Q P

The paintings in this book were done in Winsor & Newton gouache and watercolors
on 140-lb. T.H. Saunders cold-press paper.
The text type was set in ITC Barcelona Book.
The display type was handlettered by the artist based on ITC Goudy Sans Italic.
Composed by Thompson Type, San Diego, California
Color separations by Bright Arts (Hong Kong) Ltd.
Manufactured by South China Printing Company Ltd., in China
Production supervision by Warren Wallerstein and Eileen McGlone
Designed by Joy Chu

FOR NANCY AND DON

My dad, Nino, makes the best pizza in the world.

I'm his best helper.

I help knead the pizza dough,

I help stir the pizza sauce,

and I help grate the cheese.

When the customers are finished, I know how to pick up their plates

6.

and carry out the dirty dishes.

I help give the extra pizzas to hungry people in the alley who have no homes.

And . . . I help my dad serve our pizza pies!

People come from all over town to eat at Little Nino's.
They wait in long lines because our restaurant is so small.

One night a man came to see my dad after the last pizza.
What did he want?

That night my dad told my mom we would be making lots more
money now.

The next day, my dad locked up Little Nino's. Soon he opened a big, fancy, expensive restaurant. He called it Big Nino.

I tried to help in the dining room. But the waiters tripped over me and spilled a lot of food.

I tried to help in the kitchen, but François the chef pushed me away.

I asked my dad how I could help, but he was too busy to even notice me.

No matter how I tried to be helpful, I was always in the way.

So I went home.

I missed Little Nino's.

But then one night my dad came home from Big Nino extra-tired.
He said . . .

"I miss cutting tomatoes, and chopping onions, and kneading dough. . . ."

"I'm tired of so much paperwork and money talk," he shouted.
"I want. . .

I WANT TO MAKE PIZZA!"

And then he looked at me.
"Tony—my best helper!"

So the next day we went back to Little Nino's. Soon we reopened it, and the man from Big Nino got a new person to be in charge there.

My dad, Nino, still makes the best pizza in the world.

But he changed the name of our restaurant.

Little Tony's!